The Cow Said

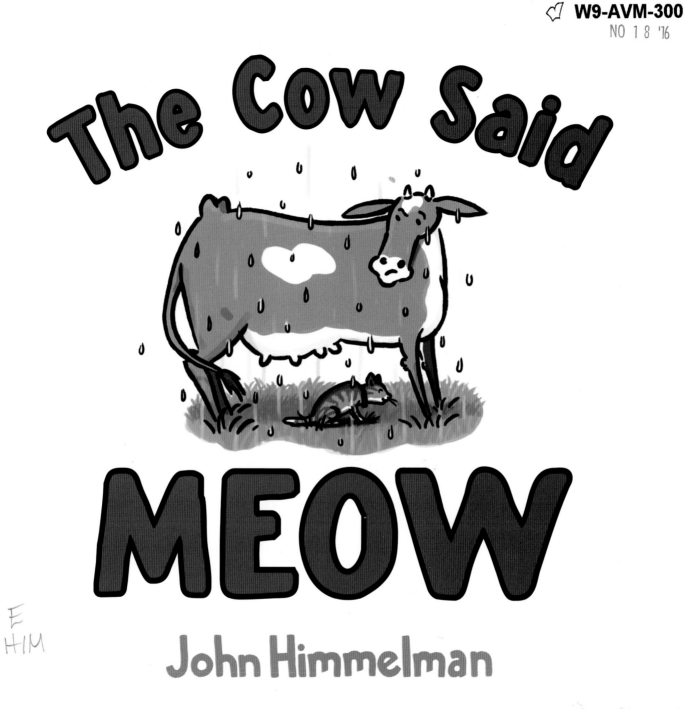

MEOW

John Himmelman

Henry Holt and Company
NEW YORK

Henry Holt and Company, LLC
Publishers since 1866
175 Fifth Avenue, New York, New York 10010
mackids.com

Henry Holt® is a registered trademark of Henry Holt and Company, LLC.
Copyright © 2016 by John Himmelman
All rights reserved.

ISBN 978-1-62779-378-0
LCCN 2015948588

Our books may be purchased in bulk for promotional, educational, or business use.
Please contact your local bookseller or the Macmillan Corporate and Premium Sales Department
at (800) 221-7945 ext. 5442 or by e-mail at MacmillanSpecialMarkets@macmillan.com.

First Edition—2016 / Designed by John Himmelman and Anna Booth

Printed in China by Toppan Leefung Printing Ltd., Dongguan City, Guangdong Province

1 3 5 7 9 10 8 6 4 2

For Betsy,
who'd be holding the door wide open
for the whole menagerie